KEITH YATES

Blind
ATTRACTIONS
GAY ROMANCE EROTICA

WARNING

This book contains sexually explicit scenes and adult language. It may be considered offensive to some readers. This book is for sale to adults ONLY.

* * * * * * * * * * * * * * * * * *

Please store your files wisely where they cannot be accessed by underage readers.

Please feel free to send me an email. Just know that these emails are filtered by my publisher. Good news is always welcome.

Keith Yates – **keith_yates@awesomeauthors.org**

About the Publisher

4Fun Publishing, a member of **BLVNP Incorporated**, 340 S. Lemon #6200, Walnut CA 91789, info@blvnp.com / legal@blvnp.com
NOTE: Due to the highly emotional reaction of some people to works of erotic fiction, any email sent to the above address that contains foul language or religious references is automatically deleted by our anti-spam software and will not be seen. All other communications are welcome.

DISCLAIMER

Please don't be stupid and kill yourself. This book is a work of FICTION. Do not try any new sexual practice that you find in this book. It is fiction and not to be confused with reality. Neither the author nor the publisher or its associates assume any responsibility for any loss, injury, death or legal consequences resulting from acting on the contents in this book. Every character in this book is over 18 years of age. The author's opinions are not to be construed as the opinions of the publisher. The material in this book is for entertainment purposes ONLY. Enjoy.

Blind Attractions
Gay Romance Erotica

By: Keith Yates

© Hank Brooks 2014
ISBN: 978-1-62761-791-8

LET'S FIRST give you a little background. I am a widower at the ripe old age of 45. My wife died of Cancer about seven years ago. It came on her quite suddenly. We went through the battle with radiation and the whole bit but within six months she was gone. It was a rough year for me. I loved her a great deal and still do. We got married young and it was not until after our wedding that I really understood that I had feelings, sexual feelings, toward other men.

I have brown hair and eyes. I am clean shaven, around 5 feet 10 inches tall and have a slender runners built. I live in a quiet neighborhood of our city. It is near the park where I often go for long walks with my dog. The neighborhood is old and very nice to live and raise a family. All of the people are great to live nearby. Everyone is friendly and considerate.

The house across the street from mine had been for sale for about a year. The family that lived there had moved out and the place was in the hands of a real estate agency. I noticed one day that the "for sale" sign was finally gone. It looked like I was going to get new neighbors. I just hoped that they would be good neighbors.

I was taking Lenny, my dog, for a walk the first time I saw him. He was carrying boxes from a van into the house. He looked like an average guy. He was attractive with wavy brown hair. He was wearing dark sunglasses so I couldn't see his eyes. He was a couple inches taller than me and looked fit. He had a friend helping him move and they seemed to be pretty busy. I thought if I caught them taking a break on the way back I would go over and introduce myself and Lenny.

Lenny and I walked through the park and he did his normal business. He sniffed, he peed and then he pooped. Over the past year or so, I had caught myself looking more and more at the men in the park. Many people came to the park to exercise. There were always runners, joggers, walkers, bicyclists and skate boarders in the park. I had noticed that many of the guys were very attractive. I found myself looking over the exposed skin of these athletic men. I was beginning to check out their arms, muscular chests, lean legs, firm butts and the packages they had in their shorts. I had not acted on my sexual feelings for other men. I was not exactly sure how to go about it. I mean could you just go up to a guy in the park and flirt or did you need to be more blunt. I watched a guy I had seen before in the park. He was running in a pair of tight fitting shorts and no shirt. His chest was broad and mostly smooth except for a patch of hair between the two pectorals. His skin was tan and his muscles were well defined and bulged as he ran. I had noticed him before wearing dog tags so guessed him to be either active or former military. I just knew he was attractive and had an awesome body. I could feel my penis beginning to respond to the sight of him and decided I had better head back before I got too erect.

I turned the corner out of the park and began the walk home. I had to pass by the house on the corner and as I walked past the front I noticed the man that had been carrying boxes earlier on the front porch. His back was to me and I decided to go welcome him to the neighborhood. "Hi there," I said as I got to the bottom of the steps. He had already begun to turn in my direction as he had heard me approach. It was when he turned that I noticed the white cane in his right hand. I was surprised to say the least.

"Hello," he greeted.

"My name is Ben," I said. "I live next door." I had raised my hand and pointed and then realized how stupid that was as he couldn't see where I was pointing. "I mean right over there."

He smiled at me and pointed in the direction of my house. "Is that over there?" he asked and was grinning.

"Um, yes. Sorry," I said. I could feel my embarrassment on my neck and was glad he couldn't see it.

"No big deal," he said. "I get that all the time. Left or right work better. North, South, East and West work even better. My name is Kent," he said and held out his hand.

I took it and shook it firmly. He seemed like a nice guy to me. He was better looking than I had originally thought. He was also in good shape. His tee shirt was clinging to his chest and his arms were well muscled and the forearms were covered with a fine layer of dark hair. He was a handsome man in his late twenties or early thirties. "So are you moving in?" I asked.

"Yes, I closed on the house a week or so ago and my friend is helping me move some of my stuff. The movers are coming tomorrow with the big items. He is in there on the phone talking to his girlfriend. I am hoping he keeps it short."

"Yes, I understand. I am sure you have a great deal of work to get done today," I said. I glanced down over his legs and lower body and could not help but notice how the blue jeans were clinging to his well - muscled legs and that he filled them out very nicely. I then saw Lenny at his feet sniffing his shoes. He looked down as if he could see the dog and I explained. "That is Lenny, my pup. We were just coming back from a walk."

"Oh," he said and leaned down to scratch Lenny's ears. The dog was in heaven as Kent found one of Lenny's favorite spots to be scratched. Lenny moved around behind Kent and he turned to scratch the pup again. Now I was getting an excellent view of his tight butt in those tight fitting jeans. They hugged each cheek and I had the urge to reach out and touch them.

"He's a great dog," Kent said turning back around to me.

"Oh, yes, he is," I said trying to hide my erection. Then I realized it did not matter. At least it did not matter until his friend came out the door.

"You finally off the phone?" Kent asked.

"Yes," he answered. "She is going to drive me crazy."

"John, this is Ben, Ben this is my buddy John," Kent said. We shook hands.

"I think I should go and let you too get back to work," I said. "Welcome to the neighborhood."

They both said they would see me later and they went back to work and I went back to my house across the street. I would see them from time to time during the afternoon. I was impressed at how Kent carried just as many boxes and furniture as his buddy. Kent was the better looking of the two in my opinion. John was handsome. He had blue eyes and sandy blonde hair. His body had a wiry build and he was not as tan as Kent. They worked long into the day making different trips from where Kent had been living to his new home. It was interesting to watch Kent carry boxes without his cane. He took his time at first but I guess as he learned the paths from the van better he moved faster. If they carried something that was too big for just one of them, John would lead and Kent would follow without any problem. I considered taking them over both a beer or two but wasn't sure if they drank or not. I did not want to make a bad impression on my new neighbor.

I could easily see Kent's house from mine. I would often see him leaving for work in the morning and then again in the evening when he got home. He would walk past my house to get to the bus stop. I often watched just because he was pleasant to watch. I found myself growing more and more fascinated with him. Whenever I saw him outside and I was outside I would make a point of going across the street and saying hello. He was always friendly and we would talk for several minutes sometimes up to an hour just there in his yard. Lenny loved it when I would stop at Kent's after or before one of our walks. Kent would sometimes have a dog treat for the little beggar.

SEVERAL WEEKS went by with me chatting with Kent and Lenny sniffing him all over. Too bad I could not stick my nose in some of the places Lenny had. I was getting ready for work one morning and looked out my bedroom window to see what the weather was doing. It was cloudy, but didn't look like it was going to rain yet. I glanced at Kent's house and saw that the curtains to one of his bedroom windows were slightly parted. I watched for a minute and that was when he walked in front of the window. He was wearing only his briefs. I caught just a glimpse of his body and it was not enough for me. I wanted to see more. I wanted him to stand there in front of his bedroom window and undress for me. Unfortunately that did not happen. I went on to work, but while I was out at lunch, I picked up a set of binoculars. The kind I purchased was for bird watching, so it should be a feasible cover if someone should find me with them. I then hurried back home and looked through my window. Sure enough Kent's curtain was still parted. I was sure he had forgotten about it. I was certain he had opened the window to let in fresh air and had forgotten to pull the curtain.

I looked through the binoculars and could see better into his bedroom. The room was dark and I still did not have much of a view. I just hoped that it would be enough to let me see more of him.

I think at this point it is obvious that I had become a bit obsessed with the man. He seemed to project some sort of sexuality that I was drawn to. I was like a moth being pulled into the flame. I wondered how badly I would get burned.

I looked down and saw Kent crossing the street. He crossed and made a right and followed the sidewalk to his door. He went inside. I waited. I wondered if he would go immediately upstairs. I was soon rewarded. I saw him pass in front of the window. He was pulling off his shirt as he walked. He paused and I realized the window must be in line with the dresser. He seemed to be looking for clothes. He was slightly bent forward. He turned in my direction. His chest was bare. It was covered with dark hair. His belly was flat and also covered. I licked my lips thinking about touching his chest and belly. My cock had grown fully erect in my pants. I rubbed myself thru my pants. I could feel my sexual energy building. He then stood there and pulled off his pants. He was standing there in only his underwear. I watched as he bent to pick up the jeans. He turned and walked from my field of vision. I waited. I undid my pants and pulled out my stiff dick. I began to masturbate. I watched as he soon stepped back into the line of sight. He was still only in his briefs. I watched and he pulled on a pair of shorts and a tee shirt. He then left the room. My show was short, but it was enough for me. I kept picturing his body as I stroked. I could almost feel his chest under my hands. I could feel his hands on me. I could feel it all and my cock climaxed.

Cum shot from my stiff dick. I could hear myself moan as I shot ropes of white cum into my hand. As I recovered, I realized I was still standing in front of my window. The curtain was drawn, but I still stepped away. I had caught my load in my hand. My palm was filled to overflowing with my milky white seed. I cleaned up and then looked back out. I saw Kent in his yard. He was planting something. I watched for a minute and then decided I needed to get closer.

I hurried downstairs and across the street. I had stopped in the garage to grab a kneeling pad. I took it to him. "Hey, Kent," I called as I entered his yard.

"Hi, Ben," he said looking in my direction. "How are you today?"

"Good," I said. "I think this might help you out a bit." He reached out and I placed the kneeling pad in his hands. It took him a minute and then he realized what it was.

"Wow," he said. "Thanks, Ben. I sure could use this." He slipped the pad under his knees and then went back to planting bulbs. We talked for a few more minutes as he worked and I watched. His tee shirt was stretched tight across his broad shoulders. His arms were thick and his biceps flexed as he dug and planted. He was too damn hot for words and I felt my cock growing again. I couldn't believe I had just shot off a little bit ago and I was getting hard again.

I left Kent to his planting and went back to my own house. I kept checking on him from time to time. He was putting in quite a few bulbs.

I noticed other neighbors stopping to talk with him too. He was a nice person and all of the neighbors enjoyed stopping to chat with him. He always took the time to say "hello" when someone spoke to him. Some of the neighbors had to remember that waving at him did not really do any good.

A couple of days later on Saturday, there was an event in the park. I stopped by Kent's to see if he would like to walk with me. I thought that like me it would be something he would rather do with someone than solo. I rang the doorbell and waited. It took a couple of seconds but soon the door opened. I couldn't believe it. Kent was standing there in a pair of shorts, barefoot and bare-chested. I was tongue tied for a minute.

"Hello?" he said.

"Oh, um, Kent," I stammered out. "It's Ben. Sorry was daydreaming for a second."

"No problem," he said. "So what brings you over here?"

I looked over his hairy chest. His pectorals were larger than I had thought, so where his biceps. His belly was flat and solid muscle. He had his left arm on the door and I could see the tuft of arm pit hair. His body was still damp from the shower he had obviously just finished and it made his hair look darker than normal. I wanted to touch it. He smelled clean and fresh and I wanted to taste him. "I, um, was just heading to that thing in the park….you know the concert. I thought you might want to go."

"Oh, I forgot that was today," he said. "I had thought about going. Do you mind waiting while I get dressed?"

"No, not at all," I said. "I don't mind if you want to get undressed either," I thought.

"Then come on in," he said and stepped back to let me into the house. "Just have a seat in the living room and I'll run upstairs and get dressed."

"Sure," I said. I had a momentary impulse to follow him upstairs. I wouldn't mind watching him strip and see what else he had. I knew that would be taking advantage of his blindness, so I just sat on the sofa while I waited.

"Would you like something to drink?" he asked coming into the living room carrying a pair of tennis shoes. "Maybe a beer?"

"Um, sure," I said.

He hurried through the dining room and into the kitchen. He was back in a minute with two beers. He walked carefully to the sofa. "Here you go," he said extending his arm. "Thanks," I said reaching. I had to reach a little further than normal as he did not get close enough. I had just about touched the bottle when he realized he was not close enough to me and took a step forward. My hand landed on his solid abdomen. "Oh, um sorry."

"Not your fault," he said chuckling. "Glad it wasn't any lower."

"I'm not," I thought. I was wishing it was lower. Just a few inches so my hand could have felt that basket. I took a long drink out of the bottle of beer. I hoped it would settle down my sexual surges. Right now I was sporting a big boner and was once again glad that Kent couldn't see it.

"I really appreciate you coming over to see if I wanted to go to the concert," he said. "It is very considerate of you."

"Oh, no problem," I said. I took another drink. I watched Kent lift his bottle. His arm flexed. I wanted to run my hands all over that strong arm and feel those hairs against my palm. We chatted until we finished the beers and then we headed out.

"Mind if I take an arm?" Kent asked.

"Oh, um sure," I said.

"It will just be easier than using my cane especially with the crowd of people." He explained as he grasped my arm above the elbow. His grip was firm but not too tight. His hand felt warm thru my shirt. I could feel his fingers touching my bicep. I could also feel the heat it generated in my crotch. He held my right arm with his left and carried his cane in his right hand. We chatted about nothing stuff as we made our way to the park and through the crowd. I found us a nice place on the grass and we both sat as the concert began. It was not the best concert and it was not the worse. It was free, so you know it was pretty dang good for free.

After the concert, we walked back to Kent's house and he invited me in for another beer. I agreed. I sat on the sofa while he brought out the beers. He sat beside me on the sofa this time. I was aware of how close we were sitting. He seemed to be comfortable with it, so I guess I should be as well.

After our third beer, I suddenly felt his hand on my leg. I tensed up. I was not sure if he had done it on purpose or if it had been accidental. "I noticed," Kent began, "That you sometimes seem to be off in your own world around me. Does my blindness distract you that much?"

"No," I said quickly. My sexual interest had offended him because he believed it was due to his blindness and not his sexy masculine body. "I, um just get distracted easily. You know hang something shiny in front of me and I will be entertained for hours."

"You sure?" Kent asked. "It will not upset me. I would rather we be upfront about it and get any problems out of the way."

"Really, Kent," I said. "Your lack of sight doesn't bother me at all."

"Then is there something else," he asked. "Maybe girlfriend problems?"

I had told Kent not long after he moved in about my wife passing. He had been very sympathetic. The concern I had read on his face had been genuine. "No, not girlfriend problems."

"Oh, boyfriend problems?" he asked.

I had just taken a drink of the beer and man did it go down wrong when he asked that question. "What?" I asked between the coughs.

"Sorry, man," Kent said his hand leaving my knees to rub up and down my back. "Just trying to understand what the problem is."

"Well, no girlfriend and no boyfriend," I said regaining my breath. I was very aware of his hand on my back as he rubbed his palm from my shoulders down my spine to the lower part of my back. His touch was generating a lot of heat in my body and in my crotch.

"You seem a little tense," he said. "You sure there isn't something wrong?"

"No, there, um, isn't anything wrong," I said. I was fully erect now and was once again glad that he could not see the pole that was tenting out my pants.

"Well," he said pausing and then continuing, "If there is something bothering you I hope you know you can talk to me about anything."

"Thanks, Kent," I said. "I appreciate that."

He took his hand from my back and drained the last of his beer. "Would you like another one?"

"Um, nah, I should probably be getting home," I said.

"Sure," he said. We both rose and in trying to get out of each other's way, we ended up just tripping over each other. We landed in a heap on the sofa. "Sorry," Kent said.

"It's my fault," I said. I could feel the heat of his body pressed against me. It made my blood surge into my crotch. I was extremely aware of him now.

Kent began to move to give me room to get up and somehow, I am not sure how, my crotch rubbed against his arm. I felt the friction in my cock and it jumped in excitement. I froze afraid to move. What had I just done? Did he know what had rubbed against him? Did he understand that my arousal was due to him? "I better get going," I muttered pulling away from him.

"Are you sure?" he asked.

I knew I had to get out of there. I was too horny for words. I needed to go home and jerk off. I needed to release my sexual tension that had been building all day. "Yeah, I got a couple of things to do before I go to bed."

He grinned like he knew what one of the things was I was going to be doing. "Okay," he said. "We should do this again though."

"Sure," I said. "The next time there is a concert."

"Heck, Ben, there doesn't need to be a concert for you to come over and have a couple of beers."

"Um, right," I said. "We will start doing that more often."

He walked me to the door and we said our goodbyes and I hurried down his walk across the street and into my house. I had pushed my hands into my pockets to help hide the erection that was tenting up my pants. I hoped Mrs. Lawson hadn't noticed it as I passed her walking her little pug nose dog.

I hurried upstairs to my bedroom and quickly stripped off my clothes. I wrapped my hand around my stiff dick and started stroking. The image that came to me was from earlier when Kent had opened the door fresh from the shower and only wearing shorts. His hairy chest still damp from the shower. I wanted to touch that hairy chest. I wanted to pull down his shorts and see just where that hair went after it disappeared into the elastic waist band of his shorts. I sat down on the bed and jerked my cock faster and faster. My fist sliding from the base up to the head and then back again. I reached under and began massaging my hairy balls as I stroked myself. My hand flying up and down my cock as I pumped it. My body growing tense as the sexual release approached. It did not take long for me to begin shooting cum all over my chest and belly. It felt so good to release that sexual energy. I wondered how much better it could feel doing it with another man.

Ever since that weekend afternoon, Kent had been more hands on with me. I mean whenever I would go over and chat with him, he seemed to always end up touching my arm or my shoulder or my back. I had not noticed him doing this before, but maybe it was just because we were becoming better friends. We had gotten to know each other a bit better.

AS I was driving home one Friday night, I noticed Kent walking from the corner. He had to pass by my house to get to his. I hopped out and called a hello. He smiled and waved back. Then he paused and turned and walked in my direction. I met him half way. "How is it going Kent?"

"Good, Ben. You just got home from work too?" he asked.

"Yes," I said. I couldn't help but notice that the back pack Kent was wearing pulled his shoulders back and emphasized his well-developed chest. As usual Kent's presence was having an arousing effect on my crotch. My cock was starting to swell as we talked.

"You have big plans this weekend?" he asked me.

"No, just the usual weekend chores," I answered. "I have some yard work to do and a few other chores."

"Yeah, my yard probably needs mowed as well," Kent said.

"I would be happy to do that for you," I offered. Kent usually had a friend come over to mow the grass, but it did look like it had been a week or so and the grass did need cutting.

"Oh, thanks, but I hate to add to your yard work," Kent said.

"No problem," I said. "I'll be happy to do it."

"Thanks, Ben," he said as he reached out and touch my arm. His hand slid up my arm to the shoulder. "I really appreciate it."

"No problem, neighbor," I said.

"Tell you what," he said. "If you don't have plans, why don't you mow the yard and I'll throw some stuff on the grill and we can have some good food and a few beers and just relax tomorrow evening."

"Um, sounds good," I said. "But you really don't need to do that."

"It is the least I can do," he said. "I would feel better if you let me repay you somehow."

"Sure, if you insist," I said.

"I do," he said and his arm went around my back and he patted my shoulder. I could feel the heat of his body thru my shirt. He was having a definite impact on my male organ.

"I'll come over tomorrow afternoon then," I said.

"Works for me," he said and he squeezed my shoulder. He then released me and he walked back to the corner and crossed the street to his house. I watched him walk his firm butt filling out his jeans quite nicely. His arm flexed as he moved the white cane from left to right in front of him. When he turned up his front walk, I pulled my eyes from him and went into my house. I would need to beat off before going over there. I would have to make sure to release my sexual urges before spending time with him.

"Hi, Kent," I said standing outside his side door. He looked so damn sexy in his shorts and t-shirt. His legs were not too hairy but they definitely belong to a man. The dark hairs made him look so sexy in my eyes. "I thought I would get started on the yard."

"Sure," he said. "The mower is in the garage," he said. We went around and he opened the garage. "Want me to start it for you?"

"No, I think I can manage that," I said.

"Okay," he said smiling and gripping my shoulder and squeezing. His hand had slid up from my lower back before touching my shoulder. It sent a wave of sexual energy into my cock. I had just jerked off less than a half an hour ago and this man was already stirring my cock. I needed to get laid. It had been too long with just my hand for sexual satisfaction.

He left me to the job and went back inside. I assumed he was working on his own chores. Those chores that never seem to go away no matter how many times you perform them and get them done. I was over halfway through when I turned and saw Kent come back out the kitchen door. He headed over to the grill and fired it up. He was going to keep his word and fix dinner for the two of us. I finished up the yard and pushed the mower back into the garage. Kent was at the grill turning the meat. All I could think of was that I wanted to get my hands on his meat. I bet it would be more filling than the meat he was cooking. I already knew it had to be hot as hell because he was hot as hell.

"Thanks again, Ben," he said as I stepped up to his side. "These will be done in a few minutes. Go have a seat at the patio table and I'll grab you a beer."

I did as he instructed and in short order he was sitting a beer down in front of me. He had placed his hand on my shoulder as he placed the beer in front of me. He must have felt me tense up at his touch. "Man you are little tense," he said. He then moved behind my chair and started massaging my shoulders. "I hope you don't mind."

"Ohooh, um, oh no not at all," I managed to say.

"Hope it is okay that I am a bit touchy feely with you," he said. "It helps me know exactly where you are in relation to me. Hearing just doesn't quite do the same for distance judgment."

"Yeah, I guess it probably doesn't," I said.

"You are tense though," he said as his fingers kneaded the muscles of my shoulders. "You could use a good massage."

"You offering?" I asked before realizing it.

His chuckle was deep and made my cock almost thump the table as it popped up. "I'm not a professional but I have been told I have good hands."

"You do," I said. "I mean this feels good." I felt him stop and I turned to look up at him.

"The steaks should be done," he said. "I'll be right back. We can finish your massage later…that is if you are interested?"

Man was I interested or what? I was more than interested and it wasn't in just a massage. In only a few minutes he was sitting a plate of food in front of me. The steak looked perfect and the baked Potato was good as were the vegetables. We had a friendly conversation during the meal. We talked about our pasts. My marriage to Sue and about Kent's life prior to and after going blind. He had adjusted so well that it was hard to believe that he was not born without sight. The injury that had caused his blindness was no one's fault. Just one of those stupid accidents that seems to have no purpose. Kent seemed to have completely adjusted to his situation.

"It is a beautiful evening," I said. "The sunset is very vivid."

"One of the things I miss," he said. "Seeing the sunset and the sunrise."

"Oh, sorry," I said.

"Don't be," he said. "Just because my eyes don't see it doesn't mean my mind doesn't."

I then described what I could of the sunset. I tried to paint a picture of the vivid orange, red, and purple clouds that streaked the sky. I hope I did it justice.

Kent began picking up the dishes after the sun had dropped behind the houses. "Why not come inside for a while," Kent said.

"Sure," I said.

"If you have a date or something…you know a club you want to go to that is fine," he said. "I know it is Saturday night after all."

"Um, no, nothing like that," I said. "No plans."

I followed Kent into the house. I could not help but glance down at his butt as we went into the kitchen. My eyes slid over those two well-muscled ass cheeks and down over the tan, muscular and hairy legs. I was once again glad that Kent couldn't turn around and see my interest in his body. I took a seat as Kent placed the dishes in the sink. I was sitting on a bar stool at the island in his kitchen. He brought me another beer and placed it in front of me. His hand was on my shoulder again. I was growing used to his touch. I actually liked it. He moved behind me and his other hand went to the opposite shoulder. He began working at the knots in my neck and shoulders. He did have good hands. I could feel my muscles loosening up as he worked on them. I was becoming more and more relaxed as he worked. Suddenly I felt his breath close to my neck. I was surprised. I tensed up a bit. He noticed of course.

"Relax, Ben," Kent said. "One of the other things I miss seeing are the signs men give off. It made this much easier when you could see another man's reaction." His hands slid from my shoulders down over my chest. His fingers rubbed across my nipples through my shirt. I could feel them respond to his touch. "If I have misread anything, please tell me now."

I did not know what to say. I was sexually attracted to him. I wanted to be with him in so many ways. Could he be interested in being with me? "Kent, I, um, don't…"

"Ben, I like you a lot. I like you as more than just a neighbor," he said. "I hope you have some of the same feelings."

"I, I, do," I managed to say. Then I felt his lips on my neck. I felt his warm kiss and knew he was having the same desires as I was. He turned the bar stool around so we were looking at each other. He touched my face with his hand. His fingers along my cheek, his palm against my jaw and this thumb brushed my lips. Then he brought his mouth to mine. His lips were warm on mine. His kiss was filled with passion as his tongue played across my lips. I had not been kissed in years like this. I had never been kissed with this much intensity not even by my wife. I parted my lips and his tongue found mine. It slid around in my mouth exploring. Our tongues did battle as his hands pulled me up from the stool and into his arms. Our bodies melding together as we kissed. I slid my arms around him. My hands running up and down his back feeling the strength there. I could feel the heat of his body and the erection pressing against me. I was sure he could also feel my erection pressing against his leg. The kiss finally broke and I was looking into his face. I could not see his eyes because of the sunglasses. I wondered for a moment what his eyes looked like behind the dark shades.

"I guess if I had any doubt about your feelings," he said and reached down and rubbed the front of my pants, "This puts it to rest. You seem to be as excited about this as I am."

"I, I am," I croaked out. I could feel my heart racing. I felt like it was my first time having been kissed. I guess as I had never been kissed by a man before that this was my first time.

He gave me another quick kiss and then took my hand. He pulled me along behind him. We walked to the stairs and he guided me up to his bedroom. We stopped at the foot of the bed and we looked at each other. Or at least I looked at him. His fingers reached and found the hem of my shirt. He lifted it up and over my head. He dropped the Polo shirt onto the floor. He then reached for my pants. He couldn't see a thing, but in seconds he had the zipper down and the button open and was pushing the pants down over my hips and to the floor. I stepped out of them and stood there in my briefs. I was nervous and excited and afraid. I had never had sex with a man before and then when you added the blindness onto that I was feeling a bit overwhelmed. "You okay, Ben?" he asked.

"I, Kent, I have never done this before," I said.

"Never had sex before? Or had sex with a man or maybe had sex with a blind man?"

"Well," I said chuckling a bit. "I have never had sex with any man before and not with a blind person either."

"Relax, Ben," he said. "I think you are going to enjoy it. Lie down on the bed." I started to move and he put a hand on my shoulder stopping me. "Let's take these off first." He grabbed my briefs and pulled them down. His fingers did not touch my erection but it popped out and slapped against my hairy belly. "Now lie down on your stomach." I did as Kent instructed. I did not watch him, but I heard him getting undressed. The room was dark, so had I looked all I would have seen was a shadow moving around. The bed shifted as he moved on it. He straddled my legs. He leaned down and pressed his lips to the back of my neck. "Comfortable?"

"Yes," I answered. I could feel his erection against me. I could feel the heat of his body and the excitement it caused forced pre cum from my cock.

He would have a mess on his sheets. He moved around above me and soon I felt his hands on my back. They were slick with massage oil and he began to massage my back. His movements must have been from warming the oil between his hands.

"Oh that feels nice," I breathed and began relaxing. His fingers and the heal of his hands worked over my shoulders, my back, my neck and down my spine. My cock grew even more erect as his fingers worked up and down my arms and then touched my butt. I felt him dribble oil onto my butt and right into my crack. He massaged each of my cheeks. I could feel his cock rubbing my leg as he worked. It was driving me crazy with lust. He slid further down and worked each of my legs. My body becoming more relaxed with every minute. I had never felt this good.

Once he had done both legs and my feet he moved off of me. His body was next to mine on the bed. "Roll over," he asked.

I did as he asked. I could just see his face above me. He had taken off the sunglasses, but I could not read his eyes. The room was too dark. He leaned his head down and found my lips. His tongue brushed along them and I flicked out my tongue to greet his. The kiss lasted for long minutes. His hand touched my side and slid up. He was touching my chest when the kiss broke. His thumb was rubbing my erect nipple. Kent moved again, his body moving over mine. He slipped his leg across my body so he was straddling me again. He was positioned so that our cocks were touching. His low hanging balls resting against my balls. His stiff cock sticking out over my stiff dick that had flopped up and was pinned against my stomach by his cock. He began working his hands over my chest and belly. His fingers were massaging every muscle and my body was responding. My nipples grew more erect. My cock began to leak a bit of pre-cum.

He worked over my torso and slid down a bit to massage my balls. Until now he had not touched my male equipment and when his fingers first touched my hairy sack, a thousand volts of electrical current surged through my body. I almost thought I was going to climax right then. Somehow my body restrained the urge to climax and it subsided but the pleasure his fingers gave grew with each passing moment.

After massaging each of my tender eggs, Kent leaned back forward and kissed my lips briefly. He stretched his body out and lay on top of me. His chest against my chest, his legs against my legs and his cock pressing firmly against my cock. "Did you enjoy that?" he asked.

"Oh gawd yes," I said.

Kent pressed his lips to mine and kissed me again. "Good," he said after we broke the kiss. My arms were around him holding him. My hands sliding up and down the muscles of his back. My fingers exploring his body. "I want you to enjoy everything we do."

"I believe I will," I said.

"Are you sure?" he asked

"Yes," I answered.

"I believe you when you say you have never been with a man before. I understand that your love for your wife was strong and that you have probably been suppressing these feelings for a long time. I want to be the one to help you explore this side of you. I want to be the person that shows you the pleasure and the tenderness of intercourse between two men."

"I want that too," I said. I wanted it so bad. I wanted to do it all with him. I wanted to be a part of him.

Kent began to slowly thrust his hips against mine. His cock rubbed against mine. It sent waves of pleasure through me. I slid my hands down over his back to feel his butt. His cheeks were tight and firm. I could feel the hair on them and the hair that grew from the crack between them. I let my fingers play up and down that crack. I let them tease him a bit and I could feel his cock respond as it throbbed between our two bodies. "I am not sure I have the restraint needed to show you everything I want to show you tonight," he said.

Kent's lips were next to my ear as he spoke. His hips never stopped moving and his teeth playfully nibbled on my ear lobe. It was so damn arousing. I was close to cuming from what he was doing to me. "I don't have much restraint either," I said. "In fact, I am about to, to…"

"Cum," Kent said a chuckle in his voice.

"Yes," I said. My wife and I had not talked much during sex. We had uttered the "I love yous" and moans but not actually discussed the act or used the term "cum, climax or orgasm" we had just let it happen.

"Then maybe I should stop dry humping you and move to something better," he said.

"I am not sure there is anything better than this," I said.

"I hope you find out that there is," he said and he moved pulling out of my grasp.

His legs pushed mine apart and he sat back on his legs. His cock was sticking straight out from him and he ran his hands up and down the outside of my legs and up to my rib cage. Then he took my stiff dick into his hands and started slowly stroking me. He was looking down at me as he stroked me. I was breathing hard and the feelings were amazing. He suddenly stopped.

"Ben," he said, his voice more serious than it had been all evening. "One thing I would like you to keep in mind is that I cannot see your face. I can't tell if you are enjoying something I am doing to you or if you are finding it unpleasant. I don't want to do something you don't enjoy. In simple terms, verbal feedback is your best way of letting me know what you like and don't like."

I understood what he was telling me. He wanted me to communicate with him during our intercourse. He wanted to know that I was enjoying what we were doing as much as he was enjoying it. "I will keep that in mind," I said. "What you are doing right now feels fantastic." His strong hands were stroking my cock. His grip was tight but not too tight. His strokes were long and steady. It was not so fast that I was going to cum but right there keeping the pleasure building in my body. He twisted his fist around my head and I let out a moan of pleasure. "ohohohoh ahahahahaha!"

"Better," he said. He then leaned down and kissed me again and he reached over to the night stand and picked up something. He put whatever it was on the bed beside us and brought that hand to my balls he rubbed them for a minute while stroking my cock. He then slipped his fingers behind them and rubbed my perineum. I gasped with the pleasure. It was more than I had ever felt before. That was until his fingers touched my hole. He rubbed over it and massaged it. The hole was already slick from the oil he had dribbled down into my crack. His fingers were teasing it and making the sphincter relax.

Kent released my cock completely. It fell back leaking pre-cum onto my belly. He lifted my legs and positioned them so my knees were bent and my feet were flat on the bed. He then rubbed at my hole again and then I felt him press something cool and slick against it. Then he pushed the substance into me. He pushed his finger inside me and I gasped. "You okay?"

"Yeah," I said. "I was just surprised.

"Am I hurting you?" Kent asked.

"It is a little uncomfortable, but it also feels…well…um…kind of good….and it is getting better." The anal muscles were loosening up and letting him push more lubricant inside and he also added a second finger. "Ohohohoh," I sighed as his fingers slid deeper.

"Just relax," he said. He took my cock in his free hand and started pumping it up and down. His fist milking more of my pre-cum from the head. "Take deep breaths and just relax. You will enjoy this. I am sure it is going to feel really good in a little bit."

Kent's dick was straining to explode. I could see its outline and it looked thick and hard as steel. It was dripping his pre-cum onto my leg as he worked on my cock and ass. Kent turned his hand and moved one of his fingers and I about jumped off the bed. "Ahahahahahaha, Aiaiaiaiaiaiaiaiaia!"

"Oh, you like that?" he said and the smile in his voice came through loud and clear.

"Oh, yes, it feels great," I said. Kent had found my prostate and was thumping it with his finger. Every time he hit that button my cock jumped and twitched and spewed out more of my lubricating juice.

Kent soon had three fingers in me and was adding more lubricant. He had my hole loosened up really well and I knew what was about to come. He pulled his fingers from my hole and lifted my legs up and back. My tight virgin hole was exposed to his touch. He moved and positioned the head of his cock at my entrance. He lubed his cock up and squeezed some more into my hole. He then leaned forward and pressed the head of his erect penis against my tight anal ring. "You ready, Ben?"

"Yes, I think so," I said.

"Remember talk to me and let me know if anything hurts as I do this." He pushed his hips forward. I felt his head stretching to get inside me. I felt his body tensing up and I tried to force my own body to relax and allow Kent inside me.

"Oh, oh, oh," I panted as he pushed inside. It took a while and Kent took his time. He gave my hole time to adjust to having a man inside of it. Once he was all the way inside he rested there on top of me. His body pinning me to the bed with my legs bent back and his mouth found mine. He kissed me deeper than before. "Oh man, Ben," he said. "You are so tight. You feel so good. It feels so good being inside you."

"It is good for me to. I never knew it could feel quite like this," I said.

"It doesn't hurt?" he asked.

Kent was certainly a caring and tender sex partner. "It does a little bit," I said honestly. "But it is getting better and it feels good having you in me like this."

Kent's lips found mine and he kissed me. His hips pulled back as his tongue slid in and then He pushed both organs into me. His tongue exploring my mouth and his cock stretching and exploring my anal depths.

"Oh yeah, Ben," he breathed as he picked up the pace and started thrusting faster and harder into me. "Oh you feel so good and tight."

"Oh, Kent," I breathed. I grabbed his butt and helped him push himself into me. My hands sliding over his body. My fingers feeling the hairs of his ass and the planes of his back. His body was starting to develop a layer of sweat as he worked and giving us both extreme pleasure.

"Oh yes, so deep now," he sighed as he changed position. He put my legs on his shoulders and began thrusting harder and faster. His hips forcing his cock into me like a piston. His dick slamming against my prostate every time he pushed it into me. It was amazing. He was amazing. I could feel my balls pulling up to my body. I could feel my cock lengthen. "Kent," I began. "I'm gonna, I'm gonna…I'm going to cum!" I almost shouted the last word. It seemed to be the trigger that caused my cock to begin pouring forth my seed. My chest and belly were soaked sticky with my load. My seed was thick across my upper chest and was sliding down the valley between my two pectoral muscles.

"Oh shit yes, Ben," Kent cried. "Squeeze me, babe. Squeeze me tight and you will get my juice." I held him tight with my ass muscles and in moments his climax was upon him. He cried out as he shot his seed into my ass. "Ahgahahahahah, leieieieieieieie oioioioioioi!" I could not tell how many ropes of cum he injected into me. It felt like a lot. After that final thread left inside me, he fell forward onto me. His sweaty chest against mine. His sweat mixing with my cum. I ran my hands up and down his sweaty back. Our lips found each other. I pushed my tongue into his mouth. We kissed as we both recovered from the experience.

"That was amazing, Kent," I said.

"You are amazing," he said as he rolled off of me and flopped onto the bed beside me.

"We made a big mess," I said.

"But we also made hot sex. buddy," he said. "Come on and lets clean the mess up."

Kent took my hand and pulled me into the bathroom. We washed each other. Our soapy hands finding all the sticky places and cleaning them from our bodies. Kent's cock started to grow again as soon as I started washing it for him. In the light of the bathroom, I got my first good look at his eyes. They were a stunning brown color with golden flecks. They didn't focus like a sighted person but they were perhaps the most beautiful set of brown eyes I had ever seen. His body was also amazing. His strong arms felt even better when we hugged in the shower. His hairy chest felt great against my smoother one. It just felt natural to be there with each other.

Once the cum and oils were cleaned from our bodies, Kent pulled me back into the bedroom. He pulled the top cover off the bed and I realized that it had been put there because Kent knew we would make a mess of the bed otherwise. The sheets underneath were clean and fresh. He pulled me into the bed beside him. I put my arms around him and held him tight. Our breathing slowed. Our bodies relaxed. "I have more to show you in the morning," he said.

"Not sure I can wait that long," I said.

His hand slid down to find my semi-erect cock and he fondled it and my balls. "Maybe just a nap then…" We drifted off to sleep there lying nude in each other's arms. Our bodies intertwined like that was how two men should sleep.

THE END

Here is a sample from another story you may enjoy:

Hank Brooks

CROSSROADS
Taste the Other Side
Gay Romance Erotica

UNCLE VIC came around a lot. Even if he didn't come for dinner, he and dad hung out in the living room, watching sports on TV. As a result, I became an avid sports fan. My mother, Ann, sat in another room reading the newspaper or a book.

Although neither of these body builders smoked, my dad was diagnosed with lung cancer when I was thirteen years old. He was a pretty sick guy for the nine months before he died. Surgery and chemo debilitated him totally, so that he couldn't work. In order to support us, Mom got a job as a secretary in a law firm.

Uncle Vic became my surrogate father, which meant I was lucky enough to see a lot of him. He took me on camping trips, to professional ball games, to my own after-school baseball games, and even to his company sporting events. He told me that my father had wanted him to look after Mom and me, and he took his caregiving seriously enough to attempt to take my father's place.

In high school, I became a party animal. I hung out with a fast crowd, and attended some very wild parties involving drugs and sex. Uncle Vic was really concerned about me. He didn't feel that he had the right to lecture me like my real dad would have done, but he spent many hours trying to convince me to take another route.

Somebody up there likes me, because I was indeed saved. By my junior year, I had grown two inches taller than my dad had been. I worked out a lot with Uncle Vic at his gym, and I really bulked up. To tell the truth, I think Uncle Vic dragged me to the gym to try to save me from my self-destructive activities.

I was accepted to my school's wrestling team. I would have been kicked off if my coach found out that I drank, smoked, or took drugs. I loved wrestling, and so I quit those unhealthy activities totally. I didn't give up my old friends. They actually gave me up. I guess I had become too nerdy for them.

I had Dad's sensuous brown eyes, good looks, and flirtatious ways. Girls came on to me all the time. I was surprised to find that I was disinterested in them. I knew enough to know that at seventeen, this disinterest in girls was not natural. I also became aware that I never knew Uncle Vic to date women either. On the other hand, I never saw him show an interest in men. That was just as unnatural in a healthy thirty-three year old man, as was my disinterest in girls. There came a time a couple of years later, when I had the opportunity to talk to him about all this.

Uncle Vic and I continued to have a quasi-father/son relationship, and I stopped concerning myself with his private life, if indeed he had one.

Like all good 'fathers,' he drove me up to State when I started college. They had given me a partial wrestling scholarship, so Mom was able to cope with the expenses. I had a suspicion that Uncle Vic may have been helping out, but I was afraid to ask.

Vic drove up for my first match, and he and Mom drove up a few weeks later for parents' day. I was delighted. I couldn't wait to introduce them to my friends and teammates. Mom was so beautiful, and Uncle Vic was equally as handsome. One of the guys on my wrestling team couldn't take his eyes off him. I could see hunger in Ryan's eyes. I had long suspected that Ryan was gay. He never came on to me or anything like that, but I suspected. If I were gay, I would have chalked it up to 'gaydar.'

School was closed for Thanksgiving from the Tuesday before, to the Monday after the holiday. I was surprised when Uncle Vic called and told me that he was going to drive up Monday after work and take me home Tuesday morning. Then he said he would drive me back to school on Sunday morning, and head home immediately. He figured he could be home by 8 PM. He asked me to book him a hotel room for Monday night.

"That won't be necessary, Uncle Vic," I said. "My roommate has a light schedule on Mondays, so he's skipping classes and going home Friday afternoon after his last class. You can shack up in his bed in my room. It'll be fun. Like the camping trips we used to go on."

"That's great," Vic responded. "That'll give us a chance to catch up on things."

I wondered if I would have the nerve at last, to ask Uncle Vic about his sexual preferences. Maybe he didn't know himself. I was certainly confused, and still in the dark about myself. I wasn't making it with boys or girls.

Monday afternoon I got back to my room after a strenuous practice session with my team. I was perspiring profusely, so I grabbed a towel and headed for the shower. I took my time, enjoying how the water was cleansing the sweat off my body, and out of all those open pores. I finally stepped out, dried myself and wrapped the towel around my waist.

When I got back to my room, Uncle Vic was sitting on my bed, at least three hours early. As soon as he saw me, he jumped up. He could see the confusion in my face, so he muttered, "I was so anxious to be with you, that I left work early."

He grabbed me and pulled my near-naked body to him. He embraced me, and I wondered if he could feel my package. I was embarrassed; I certainly felt his. I closed and locked my door. I still don't understand why I did.

"I just got back from wrestling practice and needed to take a quick shower." I explained my nakedness, which needed no excuses.

"Relax kiddo," Uncle Vic said. "I know I'm early and we have plenty of time before dinner. I'm going to take you out on the town, but it's early, and you can get dressed at your leisure."

I didn't know what to say so I just mumbled something about how nice it was to see him. I finally got relaxed about my nudity, and when we were silent for a little too long, Uncle Vic asked, "So kiddo, what's the girl situation here? Are you getting any nookie, or maybe I should ask if you are getting enough nookie?"

I was stunned. Uncle Vic and I had never had a discussion before about sexual matters. Maybe because I was so caught off-guard, that I answered him a little too honestly; maybe a little too candidly.

"I'm not really getting anything, Uncle Vic. I'm too confused. I think I might be gay, but I'm not sure. I haven't been with anyone, male or female. I'm still a virgin. I'd give anything to test the waters, and see which way I drift, but I'm scared. How do you find out if you are straight or gay anyway?"

"I don't want you to think I'm belittling you in any way, Kevin, but I find it hard to believe that at eighteen you haven't figured it out yet. You know, kiddo, before he died, your dad begged me to mentor you and direct you in any way I thought would be helpful to you. Now I'm sure he didn't have this in mind, but if you let me, I'd like to give you a taste of gay sex in the hope that I might help you make up your mind, and steer your life in what is the right direction for you."

I was more than stunned.

I had sprouted the biggest boner I ever had in my life, and I knew I would say yes…

If you enjoyed this sample then look for **Crossroads**.

About the Author

Keith Yates currently lives in Memphis, TN.

He is a fan of many genres of writing including drama, camp, sci-fi, and supernatural.

From the Author

Check my page on Amazon for Updates and interesting info.

Author Central - http://www.amazon.com/Keith-Yates/e/B005X917G4

If you enjoyed any of my books then please share the love and click like on my books in Amazon.

If you write me a review and send me an email I will send you a free book or many.
(Just know that these emails are filtered by my publisher.)

Good news is always welcome.

One Last Thing, For Kindle Readers...

When you turn the page, Kindle will give you the opportunity to rate this book and share your thoughts on Facebook and Twitter. If you enjoyed my writings, would you please take a few seconds to let your friends know about it? Because... when they enjoy they will be grateful to you and so will I.

Thank You!

Keith Yates
keith_yates@awesomeauthors.org